THE GUARDIANS

TOOTHIANA

— part four —

A Battle Is Waged

Atheneum Books for Young Readers • An imprint of Simon & Schuster Children's Publishing Division • 1230 Avenue of the Americas, New York, New York 10020 • This book is a work of fiction. Any references to historical events, real people, or real places are used fictitiously. Other names, characters, places, and events are products of the author's imagination, and any resemblance to actual events or places or persons, living or dead, is entirely coincidental. • Copyright © 2012 by William Joyce • Rise of the Guardians TM & © 2012 DreamWorks Animation, LLC. "Pitch" character design and related elements used with permission. All rights reserved. • All rights reserved, including the right of reproduction in whole or in part in any form. • ATHENEUM BOOKS FOR YOUNG READERS is a registered trademark of Simon & Schuster, Inc. • Atheneum logo is a trademark of Simon & Schuster, Inc. • For information about special discounts for bulk purchases, please contact Simon & Schuster Special Sales at 1-866-506-1949 or business@simonandschuster. com. • The Simon & Schuster Speakers Bureau can bring authors to your live event. For more information or to book an event, contact the Simon & Schuster Speakers Bureau at 1-866-248-3049 or visit our website at www.simonspeakers.com. • Book design by Lauren Rille • The text for this book is set in Adobe Jenson Pro. • The illustrations for this book are rendered in a combination of charcoal, graphite, and digital media. • Manufactured in the United States of America 1012 OFF • 10 9 8 7 6 5 4 3 2 1 • CIP data for this book is available from the Library of Congress. • ISBN 978-1-4424-8366-8

THE GUARDIANS

TOOTHIANA
part four
A Battle Is Waged

WILLIAM JOYCE

A
Atheneum Books for Young Readers
NEW YORK • LONDON • TORONTO • SYDNEY • NEW DELHI

TOOTHIANA,
Panic Sets In,

KATHERINE IS MISSING! HULKING, marauding monkeys, dozens of them, have stolen her away despite a fierce defense by the Guardians. Now Nightlight, Queen Toothiana, North, Ombric, and E. Aster Bunnymund have only one hope of finding her—by forcing the Monkey King, caught by his oldest enemy, Toothiana, to talk.

But the Monkey King fears someone else even more than he fears the Guardians, and can't be persuaded to provide even a small nugget of information—can't be persuaded, that is, until Bunnymund, chocolatier extraordinaire, tempts him with his latest concoction—a banana-infused milk-chocolate egg. The smell is irresistible, and the monkey succumbs. But what he reveals is far more than the Guardians ever anticipated. Now they not only know where Katherine is, but who is holding her and Queen Toothiana's ruby relic captive.

Pitch. The Nightmare King.

To Be Brave...

An ominous wind began to blow in Punjam Hy Loo. Pitch looked down at Katherine. She was determined not to look surprised to see him.

"Thought I was done for, didn't you?" he asked in a voice icy with scorn. "No, my dear. It's your so-called Guardians who will be destroyed."

Katherine knew that the Nightmare King fed on fear—particularly the fear of children—and so she steeled herself to meet his cold, dark eyes with her own. She reminded herself of when last they'd met, when she'd held up the locket-size picture of his long-lost daughter. One look at it had made Pitch scream in agony. It had defeated him. Caused him and his Fearling army to vanish. And his scream had haunted Katherine ever since. She even felt a vague sort of pity for him. That pity gave her courage. And she was sure that Nightlight, North, and the others would soon fly to her rescue.

"The Guardians battled you in the Himalayas and at the center of the Earth," she said evenly, "and each time, *we* won the day."

Pitch's expression betrayed little. He slid closer to her, his dark cape covering so much of him that it was impossible to tell if he actually walked or if he floated. One thing was apparent: He kept his right hand, the hand that had become flesh, hidden under the cape, and his entire right side seemed stiff, as if underneath the cape he hid a terrible wound.

He stood perfectly still. Katherine looked to where his hand was hidden and wondered about the locket. Did he have it still?

Pitch sensed her thoughts. "You preyed on my weakness, and that was very clever." He brought his face close to hers. "But soon I'll be rid of any weakness. Your new Golden Age," he added, his voice becoming a calm whisper, "will become the Age of Nightmares!"

The monkeys began to screech in unison. They pounded their paws against the ancient blocks of stone they sat upon. One of them swung, paw over paw, down from the top of the ruins and landed in front of Pitch.

"Where is your king?" Pitch asked blankly. The monkey muttered a reply.

"Left behind?" said Pitch with a hint of

bemusement. "Betrayed by his own. All the better! Do you have the relic?"

The animal held up a pouch. From within this small sack there came a bright red glow, emanating from the ruby box snatched from Queen Toothiana!

Katherine recognized that glow—it was the same glow she'd seen coming from the orb of North's sword and on Bunnymund's egg-tipped staff . . . It was the glow of an ancient Lunar relic! She immediately averted her gaze, not wanting to arouse Pitch's suspicions as to the box's importance. But, she realized, this must be what gave Queen Toothiana whatever powers she possessed. Was this what Pitch was after?

Hoping to distract him, she blurted out, "You'll fail. You always do."

Pitch drew himself up, growing ever taller until he towered above her, and then he leaned over, his icy breath in her face. The air suddenly felt as cold as Siberia in winter.

Too late, Katherine realized her mistake. She had insulted Pitch's intelligence. Drat! She should have let him keep talking, let him talk all night, give her friends the time they needed to get to her.

"But what do I know," Katherine stammered, trying to placate him. "You're the Nightmare King and I'm just a girl."

Pitch permitted himself a small smile. "That's exactly right. The Man in the Moon's *toys* are of some use to me. But the prize I seek is of greater value—*much* greater. With it I can make an undefeatable army."

"What prize is that?" Katherine asked, using her sweetest, most innocent voice.

Pitch stared at her but said no more.

Katherine had to keep him talking, she had to! She had to trick him into revealing his plan—it was vital. She racked her brain for a compliment that he might believe, a compliment that would make him want to tell all—just so that he could boast.

"You've been brilliant at coming up with ways to thwart us—like sneaking into North's djinni or creating armor from the Earth's core," she said. "Why, I can't begin to imagine how astounding and dreadful this new prize will be."

Then she held her breath, waiting, while Pitch considered her words.

His eyes lit up. Katherine's heart pounded. *Pitch's need to boast would win out over his need for caution!*

She did not realize was that her lost tooth, which she held tightly in her hand, had begun to glow almost as brightly as the ruby-carved box.

Before she knew what had happened, the tooth was harshly snatched from her hand. A monkey soldier shuffled away from her, clutching the tooth. He tossed it to Pitch, who caught it easily with his left hand. He wrapped his fist around the tooth and pressed it against his forehead. His eyes closed, and he began to chuckle with diabolical glee. He was reading her tooth's memories!

"Stop, stop!" Katherine cried. "Those are *my* memories!" But a pair of monkeys sprang upon her, holding her tight, keeping her from attacking Pitch. His eyes stayed shut as if sleeping, and he saw every memory of hers he needed.

When at last he opened his hand again, the tooth was black and rotted.

It turned to dust and blew away in the wind.

Desperate, Katherine reached for the dust, but it

was gone. She sank to the ground. She felt so lost and alone. She began to clutch the compass around her neck. It was the first gift that North had ever given to her—a compass with an arrow that pointed to a single letter N, to North himself. Katherine had once used it to find North and Ombric in the Himalayas, and now—she was absolutely sure—it would show her that North was on his way to rescue her. Together they would put an end to this Nightmare Man.

But before she could look, Pitch crooked one of his long, black fingers, and the compass flew to him. His eyes still closed, he held the compass for a moment, then lobbed it at her feet

"Your North isn't coming," he said, an edge of triumph in his voice. "The arrow isn't moving."

Pitch had learned enough of Ombric's magic to damage the compass. And now he also knew Katherine's most precious memories as well as many things about her and the Guardians. And he was quite sure he now knew how best to defeat them all.

Katherine grabbed the compass back. She stared at it in disbelief. The arrow spun uselessly, pointing nowhere. Why weren't North and the others on their way?

"They've abandoned you, their precious Katherine. To me." His voice turned smooth and cunning as he pretended to comfort her. "Your rightful place is at my side. Everyone's known that from the very moment you reminded me that I once had a daughter. I lost her, just like you lost your parents."

Katherine winced. "Don't," she cried. "Please, please don't!" Fighting back tears, she pressed North's compass to her heart. She closed her eyes and tried to recite Ombric's first spell: *I believe, I believe.* But doubts flooded her mind. She'd never recover her memories of her parents. She'd never know if they had loved her with the same fierce love that Pitch harbored for his daughter. An empty feeling filled her soul.

"You long for that, don't you?" he asked. "For the love of a parent—a father. I can give that to you. . . ." His voice was low, coaxing. "The locket—you know the one—it has your face in it now. You've seen it in your dreams, haven't you?"

Katherine shook as doubt and fear coursed through her. She *had* seen it. She'd *had* that nightmare—of being Pitch's daughter.

"You couldn't count on your parents," Pitch continued, his eyes once again glittering. "They left you.

When you were just a baby. What kind of parents do THAT? And your friends—your *Guardians*—why, you can see for yourself that they aren't coming." Pitch pointed to the compass again. The arrow still hadn't budged. "Without me, you'd be alone. Abandoned. Again."

Suddenly, Pitch swirled around. The monkeys, whose chant had been drumming quietly in the background, now began to screech.

With a ghoulish laugh, Pitch flew off, a trail of black smoke, into the night, leaving Katherine alone— more alone that she had ever been in her young life.

In Which the Guardians Fly to Punjam Hy Loo

BACK IN THE LUNAR Lamadary, North was filling Toothiana in on the best ways to battle Pitch. "If we surprise him, we will have an advantage," he told her.

Toothiana and her six mini-selves understood. They took to the sky. Nightlight started after her, then stopped, looking over his shoulder at the other Guardians. Toothiana made a trill-like noise and the mini-selves hovered in midflight, too.

"Go!" Bunnymund urged. "I'll tunnel the rest of us there."

"Pitch will be watching the skies," Ombric mused. "If we come from both air *and* underground, we may surprise him."

Queen Toothiana nodded sharply and set off toward Punjam Hy Loo, Nightlight on her heels and her six mini-selves flying just ahead.

The train was ready, filled with Yetis and Lunar Lamas and the villagers. If the Guardians were surprised to see the villagers already on the train, they didn't take the time to say so. Tall William, Fog, Petter, and all the children were aboard, as were North's elves. Bunnymund walked toward the front, North dragging the Monkey King after him. He shackled him to a door in the engine car.

"You might make a useful bargaining chip, Your Royal *Monkeyness*," North growled. "Just don't cause any trouble."

North and Ombric stood at the controls in the front car as Bunnymund readied himself near the tip of the digging device. "Let's get going, Bunnymund!" North urged. "We've got to *move*!"

Bunnymund turned to his friends. He held a particularly large chocolate egg in one paw. "It's time again to unleash the inner Pooka," he said with a flourish. Then he swallowed the chocolate whole.

North grimaced. "Oh, boy. I'm never sure what's going to happen when he goes nutty with the chocolate."

"He told me that once he grew an extra head," Ombric offered cheerfully.

And indeed, Bunnymund began to twist and grow and change with alarming suddenness, and before they could tell if he'd grown anything extra, he became a giant blur of digging. Even for a Pooka, he was moving astonishingly fast. All they could see in front of them was a blizzard of dirt and rocks.

At the same time, Ombric's beard and eyebrows began to twirl. He was finally sensing bits of thoughts from Katherine, and he was most concerned. The thoughts that made it through to him were full of despair. North sensed this too, but he had more immediate concerns.

"We've never had a crazier plan," he confided to Ombric.

"Nicholas, we have what we need. Brave hearts. And sharp minds," Ombric reminded him. "And as you might recall, we always abandon our plans and end up doing things we never imagined."

North smiled. The old man still had a thing or two to teach him.

Anger, Despair, and a Wisp of Hope

KATHERINE HUGGED HER KNEES to her chest and tried to quell the feeling of hopelessness that was starting to overwhelm her. Sweat formed on her temples and on her upper lip. She felt as if disaster was closing in, and indeed it was. The monkeys dropped down from the ruined walls and formed a circle around her.

She tried to block out their howling, but it grew louder and more insistent as the animals came closer. Her heart seemed to be beating to the rhythm of their chant.

Where are my friends? They have to know where I am by now! She gazed at the compass and its motionless arrow: North was not on his way to rescue her. And her tooth—its memories were lost forever.

She'd never felt such rage.

Katherine got to her feet and glared at the monkeys. They were spinning faster and faster in a circle around her, chanting louder and louder. She covered her ears and screamed, "Stop it! Stop it!"

But the monkeys' grins only widened. And then they resumed their shrieking chant.

Katherine sank to her knees, gripping the compass in her hands. She didn't know what to do. *Where is North? Where is Nightlight? How can they not have come to get me?* And the despair overtook the anger, overtook the outrage, overtook reason.

Why did my parents die when I was too young to remember them?!

Maybe it would be easier to give up, she thought. *To go along with Pitch and become his Darkling Daughter.* At least this terrible pain would go away. She looked up at the sky and tried to make out the Man in the Moon's face. But swirling clouds blocked him out. It was as if even the Man in the Moon had turned his back on her.

Ignoring the monkeys, Katherine began to scratch at the ground with her fingers; the dirt was soft, and soon she'd made a small hole. She paused for a moment, then dropped the compass in. She pressed dirt over it. Then she curled up and lay upon the small mound.

I'm tired of fighting, she thought. *I don't want to grow up.*

A breeze stirred the air, and Katherine was glad for at least that, at least a moment of coolness. And that's when she saw, in the distance, what appeared to be a hummingbird making its way toward her.

A Brief Exchange as the Watchful Are Watched

As Nightlight and Toothiana flew toward Punjam Hy Loo, the wind and clouds seemed to be moving with them. For the second time in as many days, Nightlight had the feeling he was being watched. Toothiana, he noticed, was glancing about from side to side, as if she felt the same. Nightlight tried to see if Toothiana could hear his thoughts. *Are you having this "watching" feeling?* he asked her in thought.

For a moment she did not respond, but just when he'd decided she didn't share the same gift he and the Guardians did, she turned her head in her sudden, birdlike way and looked him in the eye, her glorious wings never missing a beat. "I do, Quiet Boy," she said above the wind. "I've felt 'the watching' many times. She is a mystery. But she is always there. In the wind. The rain. The snow. The thunder and the lightning. I do not know if she is bad or good. But what interest she has in the battle to come? I cannot say."

The Reckoning

THERE WAS A STRANGE moment as they approached Punjam Hy Loo. Every Guardian felt it, including Toothiana. They no longer wanted to merely defeat Pitch or imprison him or send him into exile. They wanted him to die.

Because of rage or sorrow or hate or revenge or even cold, calculated logic, they wanted to kill him. It was a dark reckoning. Each of them looked for the Moon, hoping that their friend and leader would tell them what to do. But a storm had blackened the skies.

And they were on their own.

Can a Pooka Grow Six Arms?

THE JOURNEY WAS EXTREMELY swift; the first car of the egg-shaped train popped quietly above the earth near the peak of Punjam Hy Loo. North unshackled the Monkey King, grasped him by the neck, and dragged him out. The Cossack's sword was aglow. Ombric climbed out right behind him.

Bunnymund motioned for them to be quiet. And quiet they were. Dumbfounded, actually. For Bunnymund was a hulking mess, covered with layers of mud and pulverized rock dust that made him look more like a statue than a giant rabbit. His cloak was gone, torn to nothingness. But what was most surprising—the chocolate he'd eaten had turned him into a massive, muscular warrior version of himself, and as an extra little surprise, he now had six arms, three on each side.

North frowned. "This is too odd, even for me."

"Oh, don't worry," replied Bunnymund cheerfully. "I'll go back to being bi-armed when we're done." Then he shushed North with all three right hands. North thought the gesture pointless—how could they be heard above the strange chanting that echoed through the dense jungle?

They looked around. The darkness was nearly total. Not a star shined through what seemed to him ominous-looking clouds, and the wind seemed to be blowing in gusts from every direction. Toothiana and Nightlight flew down from the topmost

Bunnymund ate the six-armed chocolate again!

branches of a huge banyan tree to join them.

"Just ahead. In a clearing," Toothiana said quietly. "Katherine."

"Any Fearlings?" asked North.

Toothiana shook her head. "Monkeys. An army of monkeys."

"Our relics won't have the same effect on creatures of flesh and blood," said Ombric, worried.

"Pitch is most cunning," said Toothiana.

"Indeed," replied North. "But we can handle them."

"The monkeys are a dangerous mix," she cautioned. "Part man. Part animal. The worst parts of each. And they obey no law, not even the jungle's. They are an army to be feared."

"My army!" the Monkey King screeched.

"Silence!" North hissed. He threw him to his elves. "Guard him," he ordered. Then, tossing aside his overcoat and using the glowing orb on his sword to light the way, he stormed through the thick, steamy jungle toward the chanting primates.

The wind picked up and swirled around them. Toothiana knew the way so she sped ahead of North to lead them through the vines. They pushed past immense tropical plants and webs of vines for what seemed an eternity, until the chanting suddenly stopped.

The Guardians could tell they were edging into the clearing now; the jungle seemed less dense, and they could just make out the shapes of structures and buildings ahead. North's saber grew brighter, as did the egg at the tip of Bunnymund's staff. But Nightlight kept dim. To do what he had planned, he needed to be stealthy.

The relics provided enough light for them to see

the monkey army that had gathered along every stone, pile, and tower that filled the city of Punjam Hy Loo. Toothiana flared her wings and hissed at them. "We are just outside the Temple of the Flying Elephant," she whispered.

The Guardians pressed forward until they came to a wall of monkeys. The Guardians drew their weapons, expecting to be set upon, but to their surprise, the creatures shuffled aside to let them pass. They were armed with all sorts of weapons: daggers, swords, spears, and each was crudely armored.

Bunnymund's whiskers twitched. "Pitch is quite resourceful in his choice of henchmen. Or should I say henchmonkeys?"

North was unimpressed. His sword would make quick work of these monkey boys.

With a nod from Toothiana, Nightlight darted

past the others and disappeared into the dark. As the others moved past the last layer of monkeys, they could see a single torch shining in the dark just ahead, its flame being battered by the winds. Then they spied Katherine, bound by thick vines and lashed to a post in front of the giant doors of the flying elephant's temple. Behind her stood Pitch. Around his neck hung Toothiana's ruby box.

"One step more," warned Pitch, bringing one of his long, black fingers to within a hairbreadth of Katherine's cheek, "and I make her *mine*."

They stopped. The wind picked up. A spider's web of lightning lit the sky.

Pitch smiled a sly smile and then roared a command.

The monkey army launched its attack.

A Monkey Battle Royale

THE MONKEYS ATTACKED WITH a fury that surprised even North. The hilt of his sword wrapped itself tightly around his hand, and he slashed at the screaming creatures they descended upon them.

"Do your magic, old man!" North shouted to Ombric, hoping the wizard had a spell or two that would help combat this onslaught. North swung left and right, but he missed his mark more often than he wished. *With humans,* he thought, *you can anticipate what they'll do, but these monkeys are insane.*

Toothiana flew above the fray, expertly wielding

Ready to attack!

her swords, bucking and spinning whenever a monkey landed on her back, trying to rip at her wings.

Bunnymund was able to do considerable damage to any simian within reach of his six massive arms.

All the while, Nightlight was creeping quietly along the top of the temple, staying in the shadows. And with him? Toothiana's six tiny selves. They were waiting for their moment.

The timbre of the monkeys' screeches was deafening. And for every monkey the Guardians felled, three more seemed to arrive to take its place. They swooped down from the treetops like giant locusts. Their swarms made it nearly impossible to get closer to Katherine. And the heat, the dastardly heat! Sweat poured from his brow; North could hardly see.

And so he was unaware of the villagers and the Yetis and his elf men, dragging the pitiful Monkey

King with them, joining in the fight. Even the boys—Petter, Fog, and Tall William—grabbed on to thick vines and swung into the middle of the action, sporting Yeti-crafted daggers. "Free me!" the bedraggled king cried out, but his army paid him no mind; they followed Pitch now.

Ombric, for his part, was doing his best to calm the unnerving wind. At one moment it seemed to favor Pitch and the monkeys, pushing North back as he neared Katherine, but in the next, a blast of air sent a monkey's arrow into the trunk of a banyan tree instead of into North's forehead. Even the huge Yetis fought to make headway against the hurricane-force gales. But despite trying all his meteorological enchantments, Ombric failed to still the eerie gusts that coiled and twisted about the combatants.

And even with all their manpower, even with all

of their weapons, and even with all of Ombric's wizarding capabilities, the Guardians could not keep up with the monkey horde. It was as if Pitch had called every monkey in the world into his service.

Pitch stood back and surveyed the scene with satisfaction. He taunted Guardians and monkeys alike, enjoying the chaos he caused.

"Bravo!" he cheered as a monkey catapulted itself toward Toothiana's back. Then he laughed out loud when Toothiana dodged the flying creature and it plummeted to the ground in a broken heap.

He smiled with gruesome delight as a trio of monkeys waged a game of catch with Gregor of the Mighty Smile and Sergei the Giggler. They tossed the pair about like toys while the other elves tried to rescue their hapless friends.

The Guardians themselves were beginning to

stagger with exhaustion. North found he was missing more than he was hitting—never had he found himself in such a situation. Even Bunnymund could barely lift any of his six arms to fight off the endless, screeching horde. At last Ombric raised up his staff and called out frantically, "Enough! Enough! We are beaten, Pitch!"

"Never!" North immediately contested. But he, too, was incapable of continuing—if his relic sword had not been attached to his hand, he would surely have dropped it.

The monkeys encircled them and readied for the kill.

Pitch was delighted. This was exactly what he wanted: for the Guardians and all who followed them to feel defeated.

He raised his dark hand, and the monkeys froze.

They did, however, keep their weapons poised.

The Guardians and Toothiana stumbled forward, panting. Bunnymund had to hold up North with one set of arms and Ombric with the other.

"What is it you seek, Pitch?" Ombric asked, gasping.

"The flying elephant," he said simply.

Toothiana's eyes narrowed. "He will do only as I command," she told Pitch.

"Oh, I know that, *Your Highness.* Please remind me—what is it you are queen of? Ah yes, a bunch of ruins. A handful of little fairies and a flying elephant. An elephant that no one *ever* sees. Not much of a kingdom."

Queen Toothiana spread her wings and hissed at Pitch.

"Most articulate, Your Highness. Now, BRING

OUT THE ELEPHANT, or I'll take this child"—
Pitch placed his hand dangerously close to Katherine's
brow—"and blacken her soul forever."

Toothiana took a step toward Pitch, her swords
still ready. Her face was set; she seemed determined
to attack.

He gave her a shriveling look. "Oh, my dear girl.
Your dinner knives can't harm me."

At that moment the Monkey King wrenched himself away from his elf captors and hobbled quickly to
Pitch. "Master!" he blubbered. "You'll make the elephant give me back my humanity?"

Pitch looked down at the pitiful creature and
laughed. "No, you fool. I'll ask him to remove *all* of
mine."

The monkey looked almost comically confused.

"It's my only imperfection," Pitch went on. "I can

feel things. *Human* things. It's my only weakness." He glared at Toothiana. "You should understand that, Your Highness, being half human yourself. Think of what you might accomplish if *you* didn't have that burden."

Toothiana just stared at him.

"If the elephant can take away all of this miserable creature's weaknesses," he said, pointing to the monkey, "then it can surely take away mine."

"If that is what you wish," Toothiana said evenly.

"It's the only way you'll get her back," said Pitch, motioning to Katherine.

North, his face a storm of fury, called out, "He'll become invulnerable!"

Toothiana refused to look at North. "I cannot let harm come to any child."

Then she lowered her weapons and closed her

eyes. "Sisters of Flight, forgive me," she whispered. The Guardians gazed up at the wooden statues that ringed the base of the temple. They were magnificent effigies. Beautiful winged women standing straight and tall, but frozen forever.

"If only they could help," moaned Ombric. The wind calmed somewhat as the massive doors of the temple creaked slowly open.

At first they could see only darkness in the temple. Then the shuffle of heavy footsteps shook the ground.

The Dark Surprise
Or
All Is Given for the Sake of Pity

IT WAS TIME. THE trap was sprung. Everyone knew their part. The flying elephant exploded from its temple. Wings outstretched, trunk and tusks raised, it knocked Pitch away from Katherine and pinned him to the ground. At that exact moment Toothiana leaped to Katherine and, with one slash of her blade, cut the vines that bound her to the post. Her six mini-selves flew like darts from their hiding places atop the temple and yanked Toothiana's ruby-carved box from Pitch's neck. The monkey army, momentarily stunned by the surprise attack, quickly recovered and fell upon the Guardians, certain that they would kill them on the spot.

They were in for another surprise.

"No more playacting!" North shouted out, brandishing his swords with characteristic fury. Bunnymund and Ombric dropped their exhausted posing and became dervishes of action, knocking out monkeys by the score. The Yetis, elves, and citizens of Santoff Claussen followed suit. It had all been an act! They weren't beaten at all! The battle became feverish within seconds.

But there were more surprises yet.

Toothiana grabbed her ruby relic from her mini-selves, held it to her chest, and repeated the call she'd made only once before: "Mother, Father, help me." No sooner had she spoken these words than hundreds—no, thousands—of mini-versions of herself

*Nicholas St. North will do his best
against the worst.*

began to stream from her like waves of light.

They swarmed the monkeys like an endless army of hornets, their tiny swords and arrows slicing the monkeys to ribbons.

Pitch struggled against the elephant's weight, and from the roof of the temple, Nightlight took careful aim. The final blow would come from his staff.

Katherine knew what was coming. One of Toothiana's mini-selves who had flown to her outside the temple had told her every detail of the Guardians' bold plan. Now that Katherine was free from Pitch's clutches, he would die. In a moment Nightlight's diamond-tipped staff, sharper than any spear—and the only weapon that had ever pierced the villain's heart—would do so once more.

All around was the crazy havoc of battle. Monkeys, Yetis, wizard, villains, and heroes were locked in a battle to the death. Everyone but Katherine. She stood still, looking down at Pitch. In that moment he knew her thoughts. He knew that his doom was an instant away. And Katherine saw fear in his eyes.

There was one thing she must know before the end. So she did something that was not in the plan.

The Winds of Change

NIGHTLIGHT BLINKED. HE COULDN'T throw his staff. Katherine was in the way!

Move! he thought as hard as he could. But Katherine did not answer.

He knew that something was terribly wrong. As fast as his considerable powers would propel him, he flew. But the disaster unfolded faster than could be reckoned with.

Katherine stared at Pitch's hand. Its flesh color had spread up his arm, all the way to the shoulder. But that's not what held her mesmerized. It was the locket. In his hand, Pitch still gripped the locket. In fact, the locket seemed to have fused to his fingers, become a part of him. The same locket that she had shown him at the battle of the Earth's core. The locket that had carried a picture of Pitch's lost daughter. But whose picture would be in it? Would Katherine's face be there? Would her nightmare be true?

It took all her courage to look. And then she saw. The picture was almost gone; only scraps of it remained—Pitch had clearly tried to tear it away. But Katherine could see just enough to know that it was the old image of Pitch's daughter. She felt a sort of relief, but then she looked in Pitch's eyes again. They were so anguished, afraid, lost in pain. *He doesn't deserve to die*, she thought. *Even the worst villain needs pity. He was a father and a hero once. He did not chart his past or the present.*

Pitch is fallen.

What Katherine felt, that strange mix of revulsion and sorrow that overwhelmed her, was instantly felt by all the Guardians.

Then Pitch's other hand reached out and grabbed hers. Her eyes widened. Pitch's touch was unexpectedly gentle.

Nightlight tried to break Pitch's hold on Katherine, but before he could do so, the wind picked up again, gusts of it whipping through the clearing, bending trees in half, ripping leaves from their branches.

The sky darkened faster than any of them ever experienced before. A swirling mass of clouds broke through the treetops and descended into the clearing. In the midst of it all was a tall, cloaked woman who held herself with a regal air. Her face was long yet lovely, and years older than they remembered from the picture they had seen. Icy nuggets of hail

Mother Nature makes a dramatic and unexpected appearance

and bolts of lightning churned around her as the cloud mass moved toward Pitch and Katherine, then engulfed them.

Then, as suddenly as the cloud had arrived, it was gone.

And with it, Katherine and Pitch.

The monkey army had scrambled back to the jungle. All who remained stood there speechless. Katherine was gone! They'd failed.

North was the first gather his wits. "That woman in the clouds. Pitch's daughter?"

Ombric looked at Nightlight. He did not have to ask the question out loud for Nightlight to understand.

Nightlight shimmered a response.

But his answer was one that Ombric never expected. He turned to Toothiana. She nodded. The old wizard blinked rapidly, processing what he'd just learned. North cleared his throat impatiently. "Spit it out, old man."

Ombric tugged at his beard once, then a second time, then at last he said, "She has another name, apparently. By some she's known as Mother Nature."

Bunnymund's left ear twitched, then his right one did same. "I've encountered this being before," said the Pooka. "She's not always a benevolent soul, and she is very unpredictable."

The villagers, the children, the Yeti—all of them gathered. The Guardians looked to the coming dawn, bound by one emotion. Not fear or hate or vengeance. It was that feeling of pity Katherine had for Pitch.

Toothiana spoke what everyone was feeling. "We didn't fail, but we did lose our way. We wanted to kill," she said softly.

"We were no better than Pitch. Perhaps worse," said Ombric.

"But Katherine remembered," said North quietly.

So they stood on the peak of Punjam Hy Loo, weary but alive and certain of one thing: Katherine's strength had been greater than theirs. And they hoped and believed that this strength would keep her safe past the dawn of this new day.

THE
SANDMAN

AND THE WAR OF DREAMS

*Featuring the desperate mission to save Katherine
and the appearance of a wayward lad of
considerable interest named Jackson Overland
Frost.*

Our Heroes

Katherine

Toothiana

North

Nightlight

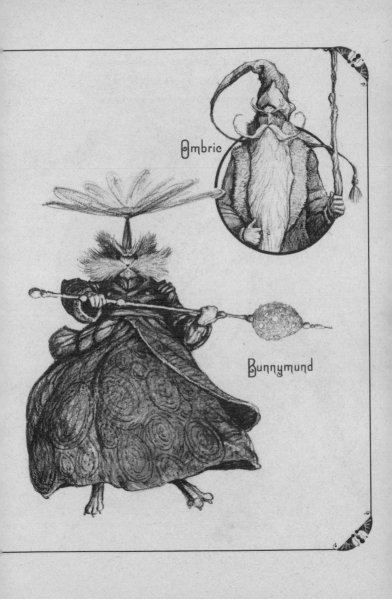

Ombric

Bunnymund

The Villains

Pitch the Nightmare King

Fearlings

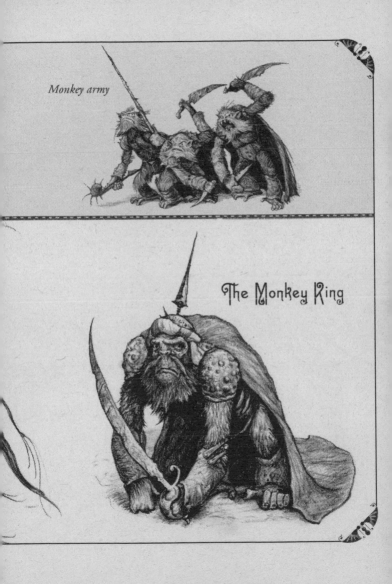

Monkey army

The Monkey King